STAYING HOME

Carolyn Woods

Illustrated by Kendall Robinson

To Luke, Kealy, and Rory
— C.W.
To my mother and little sister, Kaylin
— K.R.

Staying home feels great
But not great
But you have to stay home
Until you can go out and say
"I missed you world"
And your family is right next to you
— Kealy Woods, Age 4

Staying home can feel like

Sunshine, vacation, and freedom

Bubbles, kites, and sidewalk chalk

Melty popsicles and

Bare toes on warm pavement
Planted exactly where they are supposed to be

Staying home can feel like

Plain toast, boredom, and longing

Scratchy sweaters, hand prints on foggy windows, and lonely sidewalks

Lost puzzle pieces and searching for a new game to play

Big plans saved
for another day

Staying home can feel like

Warm cookies, library books,
and dinners together

Blankets, snuggles, and a soft bunny

Flashlights darting across bedsheets in
a brand new fort while Daddy reads

Mommy humming her favorite song

Staying home can feel like

MOTEL

A snowstorm, trapped, and waiting

Spilled juice,
sour moods,
and tangled
shoelaces

Big kids refusing to share,
while littler hands grab and pull

Grownups speaking softly in another room

Staying home can feel like promise,
hidden treasures, and watercolor skies

Dandelion wishes

Markers on a blank page,
and an invitation in the mailbox

A breeze that
rushes in through
open windows

Egg-crate seedlings
just peeking through

Staying home feels like

Love

Shared with the great
big world beyond

CPSIA information can be obtained
at www.ICGtesting.com
Printed in the USA
LVHW070705030121
675543LV00005B/111

9 780578 751009